For Emma and Evan, who have the
whole world to discover, and for their
grandparents, who make everything
possible. – KS

For Shay, his 'granpaw',
Nana and Nani. – RG

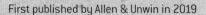

First published by Allen & Unwin in 2019

Allen & Unwin
83 Alexander Street
Crows Nest NSW 2065
Australia
Phone: (61 2) 8425 0100
Email: info@allenandunwin.com
Web: www.allenandunwin.com

 A catalogue record for this
book is available from the
National Library of Australia

ISBN 978 1 76052 343 5

For teaching resources, explore www.allenandunwin.com/resources/for-teachers

Cover illustration by Ronojoy Ghosh
Cover and text design by Julia Eim
Set in 30 pt OLLIEFAT and 21 pt Schema
Illustrations created in pencils, ink pens, watercolours and digital media.
This book was printed in April 2019 by C&C Offset Printing Co. Ltd, China.

1 3 5 7 9 10 8 6 4 2

www.katesimpsonbooks.com
www.ronojoyghosh.com.au

DEAR
GRANDPA

Kate Simpson
& Ronojoy Ghosh

ALLEN&UNWIN
SYDNEY · MELBOURNE · AUCKLAND · LONDON

Dear Grandpa,

Did you know that if you rub a needle with a magnet, one end will point to the north and the other end to the south? In the south, there's an apartment building 160 metres tall. From the balcony, you can see the entire city. There are cinemas and ice cream shops ... and me!

Just in case you want to visit, I've sent a needle and a magnet with my letter.

Love,
Henry

Dear Henry,

Tell me more about
those ice cream shops.

If they have peanut ripple,
I'll get my skates on and
be there as soon as I can.

Love,
Grandpa

Dear Grandpa,

Did you know it is exactly 2003 km from your house to my new apartment? If all the blue whales in the world made a line, they still couldn't reach me, and they are even bigger than a brachiosaurus.

I don't think you could skate that far, Grandpa.

Love,
Henry

Dear Henry,

If it's too far to skate, I'll catch a ride on one of those whales. We'll stay up late and count the stars, just like we used to.

Love,
Grandpa

Dear Grandpa,

Did you know there are
400 billion stars just in
the Milky Way galaxy?
If a caveman started
counting them 60,000
years ago, he still
wouldn't be finished.

Love,
Henry

Dear Henry,

If the caveman had a
little cave grandson,
he'd be finished twice
as fast. Besides, they
could always skip a few.

Love,
Grandpa

Dear Grandpa,

The cave grandson might
not be as little as you
think. Did you know I've
grown three centimetres
since I moved away?
If I grow that fast my
whole life, I'll be as tall
as a giraffe by the time
I'm your age.

Love,
Henry

Dear Henry,

If you were as tall as a giraffe, how would I kiss you goodnight? Don't you think you'd better stop growing before you get that tall?

Love,
Grandpa

Dear Grandpa,

Short or tall doesn't matter. If even the whales can't reach my house, I'm not getting a goodnight kiss anyhow.

Love,
Henry

Dear Henry,

I send you my kiss
every night. I tie
it to the tail of a
shooting star.

Love,
Grandpa

Dear Henry,

Grandpas are good at tricky things. I do at least ten every morning, before you've even eaten your breakfast.

And Henry, did you know, when you're a grandpa, nothing is impossible.

xox

Dear Henry,

Did you know that if you rub a needle with a magnet, one end will point to the south and the other end to the north? In the north, there's a wooden house with a blue front door. From the balcony you can count a billion stars. There are mango trees and fireflies... and me!

Just in case you want to visit, I've left a needle and a magnet with my letter.

Love,
Grandpa

KATE SIMPSON is a picture book author and an engineer with a love of facts and figures. She is also a mother of two young children.

RONOJOY GHOSH is an award-winning picture book creator. *Ollie and the Wind* was short-listed for the 2016 CBCA Book of the Year and *I'm Australian, Too*, written by Mem Fox, was a 2018 CBCA Notable Book.